A Note to Parents

For many children, learning math is difficult and "I hate math!" is their first response — to which many parents silently add "Me, too!" Children often see adults comfortably reading and writing, but they rarely have such models for mathematics. And math fear can be catching!

The easy-to-read stories in this *Hello Math* series were written to give children a positive introduction to mathematics, and parents a pleasurable re-acquaintance with a subject that is important to everyone's life. *Hello Math* stories make mathematical ideas accessible, interesting, and fun for children. The activities and suggestions at the end of each book provide parents with a hands-on approach to help children develop mathematical interest and confidence.

Enjoy the mathematics!
• Give your child a chance to retell the story. The more familiar children are with the story, the more they will understand its mathematical concepts.
• Use the colorful illustrations to help children "hear and see" the math at work in the story.
• Treat the math activities as games to be played for fun. Follow your child's lead. Spend time on those activities that engage your child's interest and curiosity.
• Activities, especially ones using physical materials, help make abstract mathematical ideas concrete.

Learning is a messy process. Learning about math calls for children to become immersed in lively experiences that help them make sense of mathematical concepts and symbols.

Although learning about numbers is basic to math, other ideas, such as identifying shapes and patterns, measuring, collecting and interpreting data, reasoning logically, and thinking about chance, are also important. By reading these stories and having fun with the activities, you will help your child enthusiastically say *"Hello, Math,"* instead of "I hate math."

—Marilyn Burns
National Mathematics Educator
Author of *The I Hate Mathematics! Book*

To Mike, Casey, Mickey, Jamey, Danny, and Timmy—
I have a lot!
—S.M.K.

To my stepson Jordan
—J.Z.

Copyright © 1997 by Scholastic Inc.
The activities on pages 27-32 copyright © 1997 by Marilyn Burns.
All rights reserved. Published by Scholastic Inc.
HELLO MATH READER and CARTWHEEL BOOKS and associated logos are trademarks and/or registered trademarks of Scholastic Inc.

Library of Congress Cataloging-in-Publication Data

Meltzer Kleinhenz, Sydnie.
    More for me / by Sydnie Meltzer Kleinhenz; illustrated by Jerry Zimmerman; math activities by Marilyn Burns.
        p.   cm.—(Hello math reader. Level 2)
    Summary: When a little boy insists he wants more served to him for breakfast, his sister obliges by rearranging what he has. Includes section with related activities.
    ISBN 0-590-30877-7
    [1. Measurement—Fiction. 2. Brothers and sisters—Fiction. 3. Stories in rhyme.] I. Zimmerman, Jerry, ill. II. Burns, Marilyn III. Title. IV. Series.
    PZ8.3.M551554Mo   1997
    [E]—dc21   97-5283
                                                                                 CIP
                                                                                  AC

10   8 /0

Printed in the U.S.A.   23
First printing, November 1997

MORE FOR ME!

by Sydnie Meltzer Kleinhenz
Illustrated by Jerry Zimmerman
Math Activities by Marilyn Burns
Hello Math Reader — Level 2

SCHOLASTIC INC.
New York Toronto London Auckland Sydney

Monty jumped right
out of bed.
"I want breakfast.
Lots!" he said.

He quickly dressed.
He could not wait
to find out what
would fill his plate.

Monty said,
"Is that my toast?
There's just one slice.
I want the most!

"More! More! More!
I want a lot!"
He pushed away the plate
he got.

His sister hid behind the door.
She neatly cut the toast in four.

"Now, look," she said,
"you have a lot."
So that's what Monty thought
he got.

Then Monty said,
"What's in my cup?
I'll swallow once and drink
this up.

"More! More! More!
I want a lot!"
He pushed away the cup he got.

His sister poured out every drop,
and filled a thin glass to the top.

"Now, look," she said,
"you have a lot."
So that's what Monty thought
he got.

Monty said,
"I see four chunks.
I like to have a lot more hunks!

"More! More! More!
I want a lot!"
He pushed away the bowl he got.

His sister slowly shook her head.
She chopped the chunks to bits
instead.

"Now, look," she said,
"you have a lot."
So that's what Monty thought
he got.

Then Monty frowned
and banged his spoon.
"My cereal will be
gone too soon."

His sister did not pour or slice.
She scooped out half
and served him twice.

"Now, look," she said,
"you have a lot."
So that's what Monty thought
he got.

When Monty's breakfast
reached an end,
his sister said, "No more pretend.
I'll give you lots,
since that's your wish."
She gave him every dirty dish.

Then Monty cried,
"This stack's too high!"
His sister grinned…

...and helped him dry.

• ABOUT THE ACTIVITIES •

Most young children under the age of seven or eight do not apply the kind of formal reasoning that seems obvious and effortless to us as adults. It's typical for children to have misconceptions as Monty did. For example, if you placed two new identical pencils side by side with the erasers lined up, children will know that they are the same length. But move one pencil forward so that the erasers are no longer lined up, and young children will most likely think that one pencil is longer than the other. Or if you place five cups and five saucers in lines next to each other so that it's easy to see that there are the same number of each, and then you spread apart the cups so that the line of them stretches further than the line of saucers, young children believe that now there are more cups.

The development of reasoning ability takes place naturally in children, and it's beneficial to provide them ample opportunity to experiment with physical materials that help them see and discover relationships.

More for Me! is an engaging story for children. For adults, listening to children's responses to the story and to the activities that follow provides insights into how children reason. Follow your child's lead and have fun with the math!

—Marilyn Burns

You'll find tips and suggestions for guiding the activities whenever you see a box like this!

Retelling the Story

When his sister served Monty his toast, he complained, "More! More! More!" When she cut his toast into four pieces, Monty was happy because he thought he had more toast to eat. What do you think about Monty's thinking?

When Monty complained that there wasn't enough to drink in his cup, his sister poured every drop into a tall, thin glass. Monty thought he had more to drink. What do you think about Monty's thinking?

Monty complained when only four chunks of banana were in his cereal. "I like to have a lot more hunks!" he said. So his sister cut the banana into many smaller bits and Monty was happy because he thought he had more. What do you think about that?

Monty also wanted more cereal. His sister put half of Monty's cereal in another bowl so Monty had two bowls of cereal. He thought he had more cereal to eat. Do you think Monty had more? Why or why not?

Your child's responses to these situations will give insights into his or her thinking. Don't judge the answers you get or try to "correct" your child. Over time, watch for changes in his or her thinking patterns. In the meantime, try the following activities together.

More, More, More... Shapes!

What if Monty's sister had cut the toast into four pieces and arranged them into a shape that was different from the whole piece of toast? Would Monty think that a different shape gave him more to eat? Here's a way to help you decide!

You'll need to cut out five squares of paper, all the same size and each about as big as a piece of toast. You'll also need some tape.

Cut four of the squares into four triangles each, just as Monty's sister did to the toast. You should then have one uncut square and 16 triangles. Count to check.

Take four of the triangles and arrange them into a rectangle as the drawing shows. *Hint:* First put two of the triangles together to make a square.

Then put the other two triangles together to make a square. Put the two squares together to make a rectangle. Use tape to hold them together.

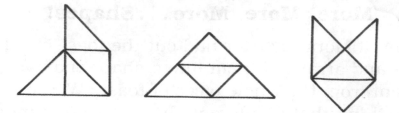

Take four more triangles, arrange them into a different shape, and tape them. (There are three examples above.) Be careful not to overlap triangles, just place each one next to another. Make and tape a different shape with four other triangles, and then a different shape with the last four triangles.

(If you want to make other shapes, just cut out more squares the same size and cut each of them into four triangles.)

Be sure the shapes you made are all different. You can test them by putting one on top of the other and turning them this way and that to make sure they don't match exactly.

When you are finished, lay all the shapes out on the table. Do you think that the amount of "toast" in each shape is the same or different? Why do you think that?

> It takes many experiences over time for children to understand that all shapes made from piecing together the same number of equally sized pieces have the same area (that is, take up the same amount of space). This idea can't be directly taught, nor should it be. Children need exploring and taking time to make the idea their own.

When comparing the lengths of two objects, many young children put them side by side randomly, and then often declare that the one "farther ahead" is longer. They have not yet recognized the importance of a common baseline. Watch as your child tries this activity, and help if he or she isn't lining up objects correctly. It takes many measuring experiences for most children to see the importance of lining up objects at one of each of their ends.

Just as Long

Here's another game to play. Take a kitchen spoon, and find at least 10 objects in the house that you think are just as long as the spoon. Try books, pencils, the telephone, and anything else you can find. To check, compare the spoon with each object you found. Is it just as long as the spoon? What objects surprised you because they were or were not the same length?

Monty's idea about the amount in the cup versus the glass is typical for young children. While you can't "teach" your child that the amounts are equal, you can give your child experience with measuring how much different containers hold. Explorations like the activity below help build a foundation on which children will later base their reasoning. It also gives children experience with capacity and volume.

How Much Fits in There?

In the story, Monty complained that there wasn't enough to drink in his cup. When his sister poured his cupful into a tall, thin glass, Monty was then happy. He thought he had more to drink.

Here's a way to compare containers to see which hold more and which hold less. You need some small empty containers of different sizes and shapes. You also need something to fill them with, like sand, beans, rice, or water, and a spoon for measuring. Find a place to play where it's okay if you're a little messy.

Now pick one of the containers and guess how many spoonfuls of the sand, beans, or rice it will take to fill it. Fill it, counting the spoonfuls. Then pick another container and try the same thing.

Test all of the containers in this way. See if you can figure out which container holds the most and which holds the least.